I L

A Childhood on Fire-Grit, Wheelies, and Wonder in 1980s

Bobby Mortimer
AKA Mort

Chapter 1: I Lived

I was born in 1970, a time of bell-bottoms, bold colours, and big dreams—but my life was never painted in the bright strokes that defined the decade. I came into the world in Aldridge, Walsall, in the heart of the West Midlands, and was the first cry in a household that would soon be overflowing with noise, pain, and silence in all the wrong places.

We lived at 87 Redhouse Lane, a council house with more grit than glamour, where the bricks held stories, and the walls absorbed every scream and sob. My early memories are a patchwork of chaos and courage. Before I could fully understand the world around me, I had already seen too much. I watched my father buckle under the pressures of life, a proud man brought to his knees by an invisible force that snapped his mind like a dry twig.

What made it all the more painful was that dad had been gifted—an artist in his own right. A stone mason by trade, his hands could carve elegance from marble rock. He built things that stood the test of time—chimneys, walls, fireplaces, even intricate facades. His work was admired. But all of that dissolved when his mind cracked under the pressure. He went from chiselling masterpieces to staring blankly out of hospital windows at Saint Matthew's, his spirit caged behind glass.

His nervous breakdown was my wake-up call. While most kids were chasing footballs and licking melted ice lollies, I was staring into the eyes of a man I barely recognized—my dad, who had become a shell. Locked away in a mental institution, he returned angrier, darker, a shadow haunted by the same pressures that stole him in the first place. Alcohol became his only friend, and his rage had a new home—our home.

There was one summers afternoon I'll never forget. Paul was messing with his chopper bike wheels, Dad had somehow escaped from Saint Matthew's. I remember the sound of the gate rattling, the front door bursting open. He was wild-eyed, and muttering things I couldn't understand. We all froze as he stumbled through the house like a ghost reclaiming his tomb. For a moment, I saw a glimmer of my father—the real him—before the front window lit up with flashing blue. The police arrived minutes later.

They forced their way in, wrestled him to the ground as he screamed like an animal, clawing at the carpet. He cried out for his kids, for Mum, for help. Then came the straitjacket. The white canvas wrapped around him like a death shroud. But what shook me most was my eldest brother. He charged at the officers in a blind rage, swinging his fists, screaming at them to let Dad go. He fought until he was pinned to the wall, breathless and furious.

I was hiding up in the Womping Willow tree, its thick branches cradling me like a scared animal clinging to shelter. Below, I watched helplessly as the police dragged my dad away. The one person who was my rock—my foundation, my stability, my everything—was being forced into the back of a police car. Gone. Just like that. Neighbours stood on their doorsteps pointing, whispering, but not judging looking at Paul and Mom with sadness and empathy.

Paul tried to run after him, screaming, but Mum and the officers held him back. We were left behind—confused, hollow, and scared. I stayed in the tree until it was pitch black dark,.

What struck me most, though, was what happened after. In the years that followed, there was always a police presence around, but not in the way you'd expect. It felt more like... a guardian angel.

Barry Dukes. He was the local beat bobby who patrolled the streets of Aldridge. He always seemed to be nearby, never too far off, like a quiet watchman keeping an eye on us. In those days, the police still had roots in the community. They weren't faceless uniforms. They were protectors. And for a family that had lost its centre, Barry was the closest thing we had to someone watching our backs.

The womping-willow tree became my escape for years to follow. It's still there right outside the house, I sometimes drive past it when in strange reflective head space.

That was the last time we saw what was our Dad, the man I worshiped and recognised as Dad died, the Dad who came out of Saint Mathews wasn't my Dad, he was a shadow of the man that I called Dad, he never recovered its 1980, I was 10, pubs became his escape.

I had to grow up fast. There was no time for childhood when survival was at stake. My playgrounds became scrap yards and back alleys. Tatting scrap metal, working in car scrap yards, earning money any way I could just to help put food on the table. Wagging school became a strategy. I didn't need school; I needed money. And truth be told, the school didn't want me either. Dyslexic, struggling to read and write, I was labelled 'slow' and singled out by teachers.

Free dinners and school clothing vouchers marked me as different. No Christmas or birthday presents made me feel forgotten. As most 10-year-olds are enjoying the freedom of childhood my world became the desperation of earning money.

I was the odd one out, not just in school but in my own family. My older brother who became a—paranoid schizophrenic—beat me senseless more times than I could count. His demons danced with mine in silence, but his found fists while mine buried themselves in solitude. He had a red Chopper bike, the one with the automatic gear shifter on the crossbar. I used to dream of riding that bike, of coasting down the estate streets like I was flying. But he'd never let me near it. He wouldn't let me hang out with him. I was the little one, the runt, the reminder of everything broken in our family.

Three brothers, John, Chris, & Paul, John and Chris were too young to be aware of what was going on back then, John was Mom's favourite, Chris Nans Favourite, Paul Dads Favourite, me ignored never feeling part of anything always hearing the voices say was I adopted. Paul and Dads bond was probably the reason Dads breakdown hurt him so much to the point of his own battle with schizophrenia stemming from that day of Dad's breaking point.

When Paul's anger boiled over, it was me he took it out on. He'd grab me by the collar and throw me into walls, punch me until I bled or fell then kick me frantically my ears rang from his shouting, kicking me in the gut he couldn't care who was looking. One time, I hid for a week camping on my own in Linley-Woods I wasn't terrified of the dark the darkness of the woods became my best friends. Another time, he knelt on my chest punching me in my face while shouting, "You're the reason Dad's like this!" you were adopted. Whether I believed it or not, I don't know. But in those moments, I believed it.

And if the world outside was tough, my own body joined the battle. Born with Charcot-Marie-Tooth disease, my feet and legs were twisted from the start. By seven, I was under the surgeon's knife, both feet and legs opened up to give me a chance at walking. But it was never easy. Falling over was a daily event. My knees were in a constant state of scab and scar. My jeans were always torn, my shoes worn through. Doctors and Surgeon's told my mom I'd be in a wheelchair by the time I hit twenty. I used to tell my mom I'm not going to be in a wheelchair they are wrong.

But the pain didn't just come from the falls or the operations. It came from the words too. I was bullied relentlessly from the age of five, even before I fully understood what made me different. Other kids pointed at my legs, at the way I walked, stumbled, fell. They laughed when I tripped over my own feet. They mimicked my gait in the playground, turning my limp into a performance. It wasn't just teasing—it was humiliation. I'd hear them whisper behind me, or sometimes shout to my face, calling me names I didn't even understand yet, but I knew they hurt.

I recall one trip onto broken glass, I had to grit my teeth pulling the glass out of my knees, knowing I had just ripped another pair of jeans open, the blood running down my legs whilst I limped home, to be honest I'd built up a high pain threshold by this point. I was more worried about mom's reaction to my ripped jeans.

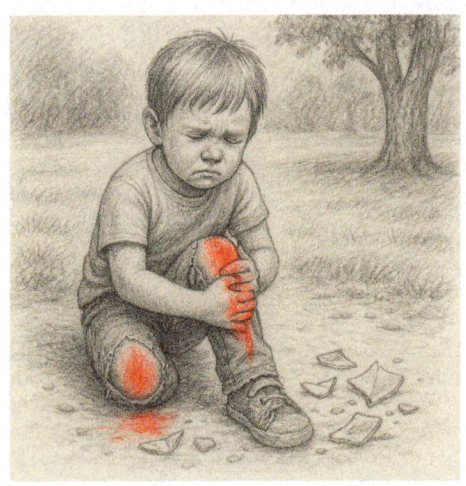

At Redhouse Junior School, I never felt safe. Playtime was the worst. I'd try to stay close to the dinner ladies or find a wall to lean against, pretending I was just tired, just resting. But even then, they found me. I remember one day; a group of boys surrounded me and pushed me over. I hit the ground hard. My knees bled through my trousers, and they laughed like it was the funniest thing they'd ever seen. I didn't cry, though. I never gave them that. I'd bite down on the inside of my cheek until it bled before I let a tear fall.

Being disabled wasn't just a physical struggle. It made me a target. It made me feel like I didn't belong anywhere. I was five years old, already learning how to carry shame that wasn't mine to carry. Already learning that some people could be cruel for no reason at all. And I couldn't go home and tell anyone about it. Not with everything else going on. My bruises had to blend in with the one's life was already giving me.

But I wasn't ready to give in. I raged against the world in my own way—raging against the education system that never tried to understand me, just so I could be suspended and go work where I felt more useful. Every morning, I got up and lived. Bruised, battered, broken—but alive. My story doesn't start with triumph. It starts with grit.

There were moments I wished someone had seen me—not just looked at me but really seen me. Behind the scruffy clothes and clumsy feet was a kid carrying more than any child should. I remember standing in the schoolyard, watching other kids laugh and play, their lives seemingly untouched by the storms that flooded mine. I envied their innocence, their lightness. I wanted to scream at them, "Do you know how lucky you are?"

Sometimes I escaped by building worlds in my mind. I'd imagine I was somewhere else—anywhere else. A place where I wasn't the kid with the funny walk, the one with holes in his shoes, the one who came to school hungry, cold, and tired from a night of dodging flying bottles and slurred insults at home. I'd dream of being someone different, someone stronger, someone who mattered.

Dyslexia played a part in a childhood already struggling; back then teachers and schools did not handle dyslexic children with any compassion whatsoever quiet the opposite, I was one of a small handful of children who were singled out, sat at a small table right in the centre of the assembly hall, with the most horrible of teachers who seemed to misplace their own internalised anger towards those of us at this table.

The Tin of Words It was public humiliation. Plain and simple.

They stuck us in the middle of the assembly hall—like animals on show. A single table, bare except for a cold red tin full of words we couldn't read. That tin might as well have been full of stones, because every time we reached inside, it hit like one. Hard. Heavy. Shameful. I've left the teachers name out of this book deliberately as this book is not a tool for revenge, life is far too short to hold a grudge.

We weren't in trouble. But it felt like we were being punished. Singled out. Lined up like we were broken. Thick. Useless. Dumb.

The teacher never smiled. She didn't teach; she barked. Snapped. Pointed. Rolled her eyes when we got it wrong. Which was often, because no one had ever taken the time to understand why the words didn't come easy. Her anger clung to us like a smell we couldn't wash off.

And while we sat there, kids from other classes would walk past—glancing at us, smirking, whispering. They saw us sat apart and learned we were less. We were the "special" ones. Not gifted special. Not cared-for special. Just the kind of "special" that meant not good enough to be in a real classroom.

I never forgot that assembly room. That tin. That feeling. I buried it, deep—because carrying it every day would've wrecked me. But don't get me wrong... it never left me.

That table left a scar. But scars, if nothing else, remind you that you survived something. And I did.

There was a large banner on the wall at the far end of the assembly hall, the sunlight would shine on it like divine intervention at least 6 foot wide with huge wording "Perseverance" for me, being dyslexic, it took many years to truly appreciate what this vision and memory did becoming a key part of my character.

I never let their judgement define me. I wasn't the kid they thought I was. I wasn't dumb. I was different. And in the end, it was that difference—not their shame—that shaped who I became.

But those dreams were often interrupted by reality. Scrapyards didn't allow for fantasies. I'd sort through twisted metal and oily parts with hands that should have been holding pencils, not pliers. Each piece of metal I tossed into the trailer was a little rebellion against the hand life had dealt me. I was proving something—to the world, to my family, maybe just to myself—that I could endure.

Some nights, when the noise in the house got too loud, I'd sneak out and sit on the curb under the dim orange glow of the streetlamp outside number 87. The cold concrete was uncomfortable, but it was quiet. Peaceful. I'd watch the empty road and wonder if one day I'd be driving down it, away from everything.

There was also a moment in my childhood that etched itself deep into my heart—one I didn't have the tools to fully understand back then. My best friend's dad passed away suddenly. I remember the way everyone spoke in hushed voices, how the air felt heavy, like it had absorbed everyone's sorrow. I didn't understand death—I was just a kid. But I knew something had shifted. My friend didn't come to school for days. When he did, he looked different—older, quieter. And for the first time, I realized that life could just... end. Just like that.

That scared me. More than any fist, more than any fall. It opened a door in my mind I hadn't known existed. A part of me started to wonder what the point of it all was. There was a time, brief but real, where I thought maybe I'd be better off dead. Maybe it would be easier. Maybe the pain would finally stop. It's hard to explain those thoughts as a child—they're more feeling than logic, more shadow than speech. But they were there. Heavy. Cold. Real.

But even through all the darkness, there was something else—something unexpected. The community around us. Despite the whispers and wary glances, the neighbours had a quiet respect for my dad. They remembered the man he was before the breakdown—the stone mason with golden hands, the quiet worker with pride in his craft. Even after he'd been locked away, they didn't turn their backs on us. In fact, they looked out for the Mortimers in small, kind ways.

One of our neighbours used to save empty pop bottles just for us. She knew if we took them down to the off licence at the Whitehouse Pub, we could get 2p per bottle. It doesn't sound like much now, but back then, every 2p was something. I'd gather the pop bottles up and take the walk, hoping there'd be enough to buy a loaf of bread or a bag of chips. That little gesture—a bag of pop bottles left on our doorstep—meant the world to us. It was quiet help, dignity preserved. And in a world that often felt like it was out to crush me, those small kindnesses were like gold.

My escape from it all—the violence, the noise, the confusion—came in the form of an old tree that stood just outside our house on Redhouse Lane. I called it the Womping Willow a sad looking tree, like something magical out of a storybook. To most, it was just a tree, but to me, it was sanctuary. I could sense when my brother was about to snap, like the pressure in the air would change. Before the storm hit, I'd be gone—scrambling up the trunk with my scuffed knees, pulling myself into the high branches where no one could reach me.

I'd sit up there in the rustling leaves, hidden from the crazy world below. From the top branches, I could see our roof, the streets winding away, and the slow movements of life carrying on as if nothing was broken. Up there, I could breathe. I could think. I could be still. It was the only place I felt safe, suspended above the chaos in a world that didn't seem to want me.

Yet despite everything, there was always a flicker of fight in me. Even when the odds felt stacked so high I could barely see over them, I refused to bow or break. Maybe it was stubbornness. Maybe it was hope. Maybe it was just survival. But I kept going. I kept living.

Because I lived. And that was just the beginning.

End of Chapter 1

Chapter 2: No Fear

There was something wild in me back then. Something untouchable. Anger never fear.

Between the ages of five and ten, I didn't just *lack* fear—I didn't even understand it. Some might say I simply stopped caring about anything other than looking after Mom, Chris and Johnny. While other kids stood back and hesitated, I climbed. I jumped. I ran full pelt into every dare the world could throw at me. Fear was something other people had. Me? I had scraped knees, bruised elbows, a busted-up bike, and a heartbeat that never flinched.

I'd scale garage rooftops like they were mountains made for me. Slabs of concrete stacked side by side, flat-topped and begging to be conquered. I'd scramble up fences, balance on drainpipes, run along ridges with nothing but air on either side. Grown-ups would shout, "Get down from there!"—but it didn't register. I had my own rules.

Linley Woods was my wild playground. The trees there were tall, twisted, beautiful. I knew them all—knew where to grip, where to place my foot, which bark held strong and which branch would betray you. And even if I got it wrong, I'd risk the fall anyway. There was something about the view from the top that made everything else seem... smaller.

Walls weren't obstacles. They were racetracks. I'd bolt along them full speed, arms stretched out, never looking down. If I saw a pile of sand below, I'd jump without blinking, just to feel that short, sharp thrill of flight.

People called me reckless.

But here's the truth: I lived with pain every day. *Real* pain. My feet—twisted, damaged, burning with relentless agony—were my constant reminder that comfort was a luxury I didn't get. Every step hurt. Every run felt like my bones were on fire. But I didn't complain. I didn't limp for sympathy. I got used to it. I built a threshold so high most people wouldn't believe it. Even today every step comes with the feeling that I'm walking on broken glass, when sitting my feet feel like they are in boiling water. Nerves in perpetual pain. At least I'm not wheelchair bound which was what the consultant predicted when I was 7. "He will be in a wheelchair before he's 20" were his words to my mom at Hospital, seeing mom's sadness in her eyes as they filled, she hid her pain trying to protect me. I am looking in the consultants' eyes at the time burning with rage, I'm not going to let this beat me I won't be in a wheelchair, mom tell him I ranted he's wrong. As mom holds my hand on the way out, I look back at the consultant with a glare of anger who is he to upset my mom.

And because I lived with that pain, I feared almost nothing. What was a scraped elbow? What was a fall from a wall or a tree? Broken bones heal. Blood dries. Cuts scab over. But the pain I knew best—the pain that never left—became background noise. Constant. Familiar. Just part of me.

Even when I fell from the tree at the *T.I. site* near the old Aldridge airport—when the branch gave way, and the ground met me like a hammer—I didn't cry. My arm hung twisted, broken. But I just stared up at the sky, angry, proud, defiant. *It got me this time,* I thought. *But I'll climb again.*

Pain shaped me—but it never stopped me.

And somewhere along the way, while I learned to bury my own pain deep, I developed a kind of radar. I could see it in others. In their eyes. In how they carried themselves. I could tell who was hurting, even when they smiled. I'd watch people closely, quietly. I'd see things most missed. Maybe because I knew how to hide it so well myself.

Scars stay, yeah—but pain fades. You learn that after a while. And when you do, you realise just how much you can take.

I didn't have much as a kid. But I had this: no fear, a high threshold, and a fire inside that kept me climbing—even when it hurt.

...Pain shaped me—but it never stopped me.

And when I wasn't climbing trees or rooftops, I was riding. Not just riding—a blur of bare feet and wheels. I rode like someone possessed. Like if I pedalled fast enough, I could outrun the ache in my legs, the tension in my chest, the world itself.

One morning—breaking dawn, sky still half-asleep—I stole out of the house before the birds had even begun to stir. Paul's *Chopper bike* was leaned up against the shed, red paint gleaming like it *knew* it wasn't mine. That bike was everything—chunky frame, high bars, that gear stick in the middle that made it feel like a motorbike. It was his pride. His territory. His warning to me was clear: "Touch it, and you'll regret it."

I touched it. More than touched it. I rode it like it belonged to me.

Flying down the streets, still damp from the night air, wheels slicing the silence. Pedals hammering under my feet, knees pumping, heart pounding. Hair slicked back with wind. No brakes. No helmet. No time for fear.

I came around a corner too fast and hit gravel. The bike fishtailed—my elbow slammed the pavement, my shin ripped open, blood immediately pouring out like a tapped pipe. But I didn't stop. Didn't even slow down. I grabbed the bars, heaved the bike upright, and kept going.

No time to cry. No time to check the damage.

The sun was starting to rise, and with it came the panic—*Paul's gonna wake up*. If he looks outside and sees that bike gone... I didn't want to imagine the beating I'd get.

So I rode like a demon—cut, bruised, breathing hard, eyes fixed on the road ahead. The air burned in my lungs, but it didn't matter. The pain didn't matter. Getting caught was worse than any crash. Evel Knievel was one of many heroes of the time,

I reached the house just as the first proper light cracked across the rooftops. Laid the bike down exactly where it had been. Wiped the blood off my leg with the hem of my shirt. Limped inside like nothing happened.

Not a word said. Not a bruise mentioned.

That was the thing about growing up the way I did—you learned early how to carry pain quiet. You could be bleeding, broken, shaking—but you still showed up, still smiled, still took the hits and kept going.

Fear didn't have a place in my world. I had no room for it. I was too busy outrunning it.

I remember one sunny afternoon backing hot heatwave, I'm on my own as I often was, walking with purpose but no destination holding a stick, finding the tallest tree, I walked for hours. No destination, no plan—just my feet carrying me deeper into Linley Woods like they knew where I needed to go before I did.

I was angry. Not the kind of angry you shout and stomp about. The kind that simmers. That lives in your bones. That builds up like pressure in a bottle with no cap. Angry at the world, at the weight of things no kid should have to carry. Angry at being misunderstood. At being broken in ways no one could see. At being forgotten.

The woods became my escape. My therapist. My hiding place.

No voices. No noise but the wind and birds and the crunch of leaves underfoot. Sometimes I'd kick at branches or throw rocks just to feel something move. Most times I just walked. Alone. Always alone.

And then there was *the tallest tree*.

The tallest one in the whole woods. Towering, jagged, defiant. It must've been forty feet tall, maybe more, its trunk thick and ancient, stretching far above everything else like it was trying to escape the earth.

I climbed it without thinking. Without stopping. Without looking down.

Higher and higher—hands gripping bark that scraped my skin raw, feet searching for holds, legs shaking not from fear, but from fury. Halfway up and I should've stopped, but I didn't. I couldn't. I needed to reach the top. Needed to get as far away from everything down below as I could.

By the time I reached the highest branches, they were thin, fragile, bending under my weight, creaking like they were about to snap. The tree swayed with the wind, and I swayed with it, clinging on with white knuckles, chest heaving, eyes locked on the horizon.

From up there, I could see everything. The industrial estate beyond the woods. The rooftops of Aldridge. The slow-moving clouds. The sun bleeding through the trees.

And in that moment, I felt something strange. Not peace. Not clarity. But something close to *freedom*. No fear, peace. Because I wasn't scared to fall. Not even a little.

If I slipped, if the branch gave way, if I disappeared into the air and never hit the ground again—that was okay. That was *more than* okay. The worst that could happen was I'd be gone. And honestly, that didn't sound so bad.

Gone meant no more pain. No more aching feet. No more screaming behind closed doors. No more being labelled, pointed at, punished for a brain that didn't work the way the world wanted it to or deformed feet. Gone meant silence. Stillness. An end. And part of me—sat up there, branches shaking, breath cold—wanted that.

Not because I didn't want to live. But because I didn't know how to keep living with so much hurt and no one seeing it. Because when you live with pain every day—physical, emotional, both—it starts to feel like the world has stopped noticing you. Like you've become invisible, even to the people who are supposed to care.

And when you're somewhere between five and eight years old and already wondering whether you'd be missed... that does something to you.

But I didn't fall. Something in me held on. Something stubborn. Something angry. Maybe it was survival. Maybe it was spite. Maybe it was the same wild thing that made me climb rooftops and jump from walls and race Chopper bikes through the morning light with blood running down my legs.

Whatever it was—it kept me alive. It was hours before I climbed back down. One branch at a time hands slipping from one branch to another. Quiet. Changed. The pain didn't vanish. The anger didn't burn out. But for the first time, I'd looked it all in the eye—from the top of the world—and I didn't flinch.

And that... that mattered. Picking up some broken glass off the woodland floor, I carved my initials into the tree, marking my territory marking my dance with the devil.

The woods gave me space when I needed to breathe, but sometimes I needed to disappear entirely. There was a place in Linley Woods we called the "39 Steps." Or something like that, an old, crumbling staircase that seemed to lead straight into the earth's belly. No signs, no warnings—just moss-covered steps disappearing into darkness. Some form of old coal mine pit entrance.

I dared myself to go down, with my unsteady feet, each step a test of courage. The air grew colder with each descent, the light fading, replaced by the damp smell of earth and something ancient. At the bottom, a rusted gate barred further passage, but that didn't stop our imaginations from running wild. Emerging back into the sunlight, heart pounding, feeling like a conqueror of some forgotten world. Those steps were more than just a physical challenge; they were a rite of passage, a testament to my fearless youth.

Because I lived with pain. My feet were a constant war zone. Twisted. Burning. Every step was a small act of defiance. And I never let it show. High pain threshold? I lived there. Cuts, bruises, broken bones—they were nothing compared to the pain that never left every step feeling like an electric shock in my feet.

That's when I'd head over to the *T.I.*, what was the old Aldridge Airfield. A forgotten place with the bones of war still buried in its soil. In the far corner, past the clubhouse we called *Green Acres*, through the overgrowth and broken fence lines, was an air raid shelter—half sunken into the ground, swallowed by time. That shelter became my den. My bunker. My hideaway.

I'd climb down inside it, cold air meeting my skin like a handshake from the past. Concrete walls lined with moss, the kind of darkness that made sound echo differently. I'd crouch low, pile up some sticks, strike a match, and light a small fire—just enough to feel alive in the silence. I'd sit for hours down there, warm in the orange glow, the flicker on the damp walls keeping me company better than most people ever had.

From time to time, I'd pop up like a fox out of its hole, scan the distance. I could see people far off—walking dogs, playing on the field, clueless to my presence. I liked it that way. Hidden but not lost. Watching but not watched.

Eventually, boredom or hunger would nudge me out of hiding. I'd make my way quietly to the tall wooden fence behind *Green Acres*, a solid six-foot barrier between me and opportunity. I'd scale it in one fluid motion, like I'd done it a hundred times—because I had.

Behind the fence, neatly stacked in pop bottle crates, were old glass pop bottles—the good kind, worth 2p each if you returned them. Five bottles in my arms, I was over the fence and back in minutes, landing with a thud, adrenaline buzzing in my fingers.

I took them straight to the off-licence, handed them over like treasure, and walked out with ten pence jingling in my pocket—a fortune in those days. Enough for a packet of crisps, some chewy sweets, and a box of matches. Always the matches.

I was on top of the world walking back, head down, hands in pockets, already imagining the fire crackling again, the sweet-salt tang of crisps on my tongue, sugar buzzing behind my teeth. I didn't need company. I had the fire. The stillness. My thoughts.

And then fate added a twist.

Lying half-buried near the shelter was a squashed cigarette packet. Ten fags printed on the side, but when I opened it, just a few remained—crumpled but still smokeable. My heart kicked up. Not fear. Excitement. Curiosity.

Back down in the shelter, I added a few more twigs to the fire, the smoke curling upward like it was whispering secrets to the sky. I sat cross-legged, peering into the dark tunnel that stretched away from me, then pulled out a cigarette. I struck a match. Watched the flame dance.

One drag. One puff. Fire in my throat. I choked. Coughed. Spluttered so hard I thought I'd vomit. My head spun, eyes watered. I threw the fag to the dirt and stomped it out like it had personally betrayed me. Just two drags on the fag made me dizzy.

That was enough. One taste of it and I knew—I wasn't built for that kind of habit. The others I ditched deep in the shelter, left them to rot with the ghosts.

I stayed down there a while longer, letting the fire settle, the sting fade from my lungs. I munched crisps, chewed through sweets, and listened to the silence like it was music written just for me. There, in that old shelter, I was completely alone—but not lonely. Not really. I'd made peace with my own company. It was safer than most people. Quieter. Less to prove. Less to lose.

The next night, I was out late. Nothing unusual about that. Sat on the front doorstep, Nan was round the house with Nan, Chris, Mon John, Paul in the house telly loud hearing them talking laughing not even noticing I'm not there.

It was one of those summer nights when the air still holds the heat from the day, but there's a breeze of summer cut grass rolling through like the wind itself needs to cool off. Everything was quiet. The kind of quiet that settles into your bones and makes you feel like the world has finally gone to sleep without you.

I was sat on the doorstep of our house, staring straight ahead at the 6-foot brick wall opposite. That wall always called to me. Sturdy, weathered, and full of broken bricks that made perfect climbing holes. I didn't think. I just stood up and walked over.

Climbing came easy by then. I clawed my way up, fingers in the cracks, toes finding old mortar edges, and in seconds I was standing tall—on the roof of the entryway that connected our street. From up there, everything looked different. The rooftops stretched out like patchwork. The streetlights painted golden circles on the pavement below. My world but flipped sideways. It felt almost peaceful. Like being above the noise of real life. I'm nothing taller than 2 ft tall at this point in life, around 5 or 6 years old.

After pacing along the edge for a while, I had a genius idea: *climb down the other side into our back garden.* But what seemed easy in my head turned out to be anything but. The drop was further than I thought—five feet, maybe more. And what I didn't see in the dark was the pile of broken bricks waiting beneath me like jagged teeth.

I landed hard. No time to twist or catch myself. Just *thud*—straight down into sharp rubble. My chin hit something solid. My legs scraped. My arms tore open. Blood was everywhere. It wasn't like a little cut. This was *blood*. Real and fast, pouring from elbows, shins, chin, head, mixing with dirt. There was a deep gash on my head just above my left eye which large a scar remains from today.

But still, I didn't scream. I didn't shout. Not a sound.

I just sat there, hunched in the rubble, teeth clenched so hard they ached. Holding it all in. Swallowing the pain. That was the rule. No noise. No weakness. No attention. Time stretched. Minutes, maybe hours. I don't really know. I just remember the smell of blood and dust. The stillness of it all.

Eventually, I got up. Limped through the garden like a ghost, dragging one foot behind me, and curled up behind the apple tree at the very end of the back garden. My safe spot. My one of many hiding places.

I sat there alone, sticky with blood, waiting. And slowly, like always, the bleeding stopped. The cuts hardened. The sting dulled. And the pain—*the pain always faded.*

That was something I learned early. Blood dries up. Pain dissolves. Scars stay, sure—but they don't scream like they did on day one. They go quiet. And so did I. Because sometimes falling isn't the worst thing. It's the silence that follows—the long, lonely quiet when you realise no one's coming. No one saw. No one will ask.

So, you pick yourself up. And you carry on, wiping the dust off as if it never happened. That's just how it went and how I lived.

Growing up through the 70's and 80's It was a different time.

We played out till the streetlights came on. No mobiles. No internet. Just bruised knees, gravel in our hands, and scabs we didn't bother picking. We'd swap stickers, climb trees, dare each other to do stupid things. Independence wasn't taught. It was earned. Earned by falling off bikes, sneaking out windows, jumping off sheds. By getting back up without a fuss.

If you were hurting, you hid it. If you were different, you got labelled. If you couldn't read fast or spell like the others, they called you slow. Dumb. And they put you on display like a warning.

But the '80s made us tough. Not just on the outside—but in the quiet places inside. We learned to get on with it. Learned to carry what we couldn't drop.

And me? I learned how to survive in plain sight. No one noticed the scruffy kid who looked normal when bloody, bruised in ripped clothes.

End of Chapter 2

Chapter 3 Fun

There was a spot under the road bridge, just past the bend where the train track runs along the edge of Linley Woods. Hidden from sight. Perfect.

You wouldn't even know it was there unless you were looking for it. A few pallets, some old tyres, scraps of carpet—junk to anyone else, but to me, it was a fortress. A den. Mine.

Built it low, deep under the bridge where the concrete arms held up the road above. Trucks, lorries, cars—all roaring across without knowing I was underneath, pressed into the ribs of the earth. When they passed over, the whole thing would shake and rumble like thunder in a cage. I'd lie there, eyes closed, feeling the vibration in my bones, heart thudding like a second engine.

And then the trains would come.

You'd hear them long before they appeared—the distant clatter, the low metal growl growing louder, closer. I'd sit at the edge, just thirty feet above the track, behind a patch of thick brambles that shielded the view. Close enough to see the driver's face blur past. Close enough to feel the heat off the wheels.

The coal trains were the best. Massive monsters, so heavy they seemed to tear the ground apart as they passed. I'd wait for them. Watch the blur of steel and soot. When the train was gone, sometimes it left behind a little chunk of coal—like a prize. I'd scramble down, grab it like it was gold. In a way, it was. I knew the heat it could give off on a fire. I knew what it meant to be warm when the house was cold.

It was strange—how I could feel more alive down there, half-buried under the road, than anywhere else. Just me, the shaking of the bridge, the wind rushing past with the trains.

That track ran right behind Redhouse Junior School. I'd sit in class, bored, lost in a sea of chalk and red pens, and then hear it—the train. That same train that passed me in my den. I'd watch the others barely notice. But I knew it. That was *my* train. My secret world rattling past behind their backs.

Building dens wasn't just fun. It was survival. It was adrenaline. It was creating something from nothing. A space that was mine, when so much of life wasn't. No rules. No shouting. No teachers, no labels. Just danger and quiet and the rhythm of passing machines.

If you'd asked me what freedom looked like back then, I'd have told you: it looked like pallets under a bridge, soot on your hands, and the sound of a train screaming past like it was trying to outrun the world.

One long summer, the whole world was about the raft.

Back of Redhouse Lane, just past the industrial estate, there was a stretch of canal bordered by brambles and small woods. Quiet. Forgotten. Perfect for hiding. I'd built a den back there, tucked away behind a wall of thorns—so well hidden no one would find it unless they *really* knew what to look for. The raft was my project. Four plastic drums, one battered pallet, some rope knotted from God knows what. That was it. A broken plank for a paddle. Built it myself. Got it floating. Sat on the water like a dream. I'd push off slow and drift to the other bank, nothing but the splash of water and the sound of the wind in the reeds.

Then they showed up.

Bigger lads. Loud. Older. I knew the type—trouble before they opened their mouths. My senses kicked off like sirens. Years of Paul's moods had wired me like Spiderman. I could feel danger before it arrived. I played it cool. Let them mess about on the raft. Didn't say a word about the den hidden in the brambles. Didn't flinch when they looked me up and down—raw knees, scruffy clothes, holes in my jeans, that look like I didn't belong anywhere.

Then it turned. Two of them started shoving me around. The other two dragged my raft out of the water and started smashing it up. Laughing while they did it. A few kicks. A punch. Another laugh.

But honestly? I didn't care.

There was so much other shit going wrong in my life, they couldn't touch me with that. They thought they were breaking me. All they broke was a pallet and a few ropes. They ran off down the canal, back toward Rushall, still laughing. And I wiped the blood from my face, sat with it for a while, then started planning the rebuild. That's how it was for me. You knock me down, I get back up. No drama. No tears. Just *more fire*.

I built a new raft. It wasn't as good—the pallet was weaker, rope was old—but it floated. I pushed off again, determined, hands in the water for paddles, body shifting to balance the wobble. Then it happened. One of the drums slipped out from under. The raft jolted. I leaned the other way, frantic, trying to steer, trying to level out—but the raft had its own plan. It tilted harder, the water rushing up beneath me.

I remember the sky. Blue. Perfect. Upside down. Then the fall. I hit the canal hard—flat, full, arms wide. The water swallowed me. And here's the thing: I wasn't scared. It was quiet. Still. Like the whole world went into slow motion. I was under, deep, eyes open, seeing reeds and shadows. I could see the raft floating off, too far to reach. I reached for the edge but came up short. Still no panic. Just calm. It should've been the end. No one around. Just me, a dot of a kid, water closing in. But something kicked in—instinct, defiance, maybe something bigger.

I pushed. Kicked. My head broke the surface, just enough to breathe. I grabbed at the reeds, missed, grabbed again, caught one. Then I saw it—a drum floating loose, just ahead. I got to it. Held it tight. Kicked with

everything I had until I drifted to the far side. I crawled out soaked, shaking, lungs burning—but alive. Made it to the den and sat there under the brambles. Soaking wet. Cuts stinging. The sun dipping low in the sky.

And then I heard them.

Voices. Laughter. The stink of fag smoke. I didn't move. Just crawled further into my hiding place. They were back—the same lads. Looking around, confused, searching. They hung by the bridge for ages. I stayed still watching, listening. They dragged what was left of my raft out of the water and smashed it properly this time. Then they left. I waited until the silence returned. Crawled out slow. Climbed back into the den. The light was gold now. That end-of-day kind of glow. Smelled like warm dirt and canal water.

And then I saw it. Folded near the den entrance. Brown. Crumpled. Money. A tenner. Then another tenner. Twenty quid. *That's what they were looking for.* Their loss. Call it payback. Call it the universe keeping score. Or maybe just my guardian angel slipping a bit of balance back into the scales. They didn't hurt me. Not really. Their kicks were nothing. I'd taken worse from Paul before breakfast. Without knowing it, he'd toughened me up. Tough enough to take it. Tough enough to keep going.

I went home. Mom looked the same as always sad behind her smile sadness behind her eyes, trying to hold it together. I handed her the notes. "Here Mom... I earned this." She looked at me like she didn't know what to say. Her hands shaking, eyes filling, but no words. She pulled me into the warmest hug I'd had in weeks. She tried to give the money back.

I ran. Out the back door. Down the alley. Up the womping willow. That branch—*my* branch—was waiting. By now, the moon was out. Big. Bright. I sat up there, soaking in the night, clothes stiff with dried canal water, body aching, knuckles bruised, but I felt electric. Alive. Unbreakable. No fear. No regrets.

Just me. But now I'm different more confident, guess what Bobby you can swim.

Freedom in its most fearless form, Rope swings were our rides to freedom. So much fun for free, all it cost was the guts to get on.

All it took was a few lengths of rope from a skip—frayed, stiff, sometimes half-burnt—and something to tie it to. A knotted branch. A rusty car tyre. Anything strong enough to carry the weight of a kid throwing himself into the sky. The hunt was always the best bit. Searching for *the* tree. The perfect one. Tall, thick-limbed, with a strong anchor point and a drop below to make your stomach flip. Once we found it, that tree wasn't just a tree anymore—it became a landmark. A meeting point. A launchpad. Home base for every daredevil and dreamer in the neighbourhood.

We left our mark all over the place. Linley Woods. Kendal's Farm. The TI Woods. Anker Meadow. If you knew where to look, you'd find our swings—and more often than not, one of my dens hidden somewhere nearby, like a secret waiting to be found. Most of the gear came from skips. Rope, tyres, sometimes even planks we'd punch holes in and thread the rope through. Some days I felt like a scrap-yard inventor, pulling junk from skips on Redhouse Industrial and turning it into something that made kids laugh until their faces hurt.

But the best swings? The *real* ones? They came with danger.

The ones that swung out over a canal, where the water below looked like ink. The ones that arced across massive pits left behind by old construction sites. The ones we tied to trees hanging over railway lines—yeah, we were that stupid. And the ones where you couldn't see the bottom, just swung into the void and hoped your grip held. The higher the swing, the more the thrill. The more the danger, the more that would turn up.

There was always that moment right at the top of the arc—just before gravity pulled you back—where you felt weightless. Like nothing mattered. No pain. No noise. Just wind in your ears and the whole world below your feet. We didn't have theme parks. We had rope swings. We didn't have money. We had guts. And we didn't need permission. We just needed a rope, a tree, and enough courage to take that first leap.

It was a sunny afternoon, and for once, things felt simple. Me, JC, and RC—just three kids mucking about in Linley Woods. We were laughing, taking turns on the rope swing I'd set up a few weeks earlier. I'd found the tree myself. Found the rope. Built the swing. That was mine. And close by, buried behind thick brush and brambles, I had a den no one knew about. My private outpost. My bolt hole. Every now and then, I'd glance toward it—just to know it was there. Just to know I had an escape route.

Then I heard them. Tyres crunching over roots and dry leaves. Five or six older lads came scrambling round the corner on their bikes, like a gang of trouble arriving on cue. And right there at the front—Paul. His red Chopper bike. My gut turned. Paul and his mates jumped off their bikes, the others circling around, throwing banter, lighting fags, kicking at tree roots like they

owned the woods. Paul didn't even look at me. Not a nod. Not a glance. Like I didn't exist. You'd think being his brother might mean something. It didn't. Not with Paul. I locked my eyes on his, trying to read him. Trying to figure out what mood he was in. That blankness—like glass, like nothing behind the eyes—was familiar. My senses told me I wasn't getting a beating today. *But I also knew how fast things could flip.*

He was standing on the swing now, arms stretched out, swinging like a lunatic, wild grin on his face. That was Paul. Always pushing it further. Always right at the edge. Then I saw it—his face changed. One of his mates shouted something, and I saw the shift. That moment. The one I'd seen too many times before. That twitch in the jaw. The way his eyes went distant. Like a fuse just lit.

That's when I knew I had to go.

I tugged JC's arm. "We need to go," I muttered. He didn't move. RC looked at me like I was soft. "We're staying. You go." I noticed a couple of the older lads messing with Paul's bike—sitting on it, messing with the gear stick, laughing about how fast it was. Paul's face got darker. I hovered about ten feet away, pretending to look for a stick, staying loose, staying ready. Then it kicked off. Paul jumped off the swing mid-swing, screaming—"Get the f**k off my bike!" Everyone turned to look.

That was my moment.

I bolted. Ran like I'd been lit on fire. Through the woods, away from the den—didn't want to lead them there. I sprinted straight for the barbed wire fence, faster than my feet could keep up. The wire scratched me up, but I didn't care. Paul's fists hurt worse. I was over. Into the open field. Then toward the railway. Under the track fence. Sliding down the embankment on my knees, ripping off half-healed scabs, fresh blood running. Didn't slow me down. Nothing would.

Paul was the one person I truly feared. Not because he shouted—but because when he kicked off, there was nothing behind his eyes. No mercy. Just blank rage. And I was always the closest target. I jumped the rails, didn't even check for trains. Up the other side. Under another fence. Then stopped. Checked.

No sound. No one chasing. I crept back to the den. Slipped under the brambles. Curled into the shadows just beneath the bridge. Lorries and cars thundered across the road above. The whole world rolling past without a clue I was there, heart hammering against my ribs. I sat there for what felt like hours. Let the adrenaline settle. Eventually, I headed home. Slowly.

Found a can in the road. Kicked it along the path as I walked—metal on concrete echoing with each step. One kid, one can, rattling his way back to the edge of everything. From the top of Redhouse Lane I saw it—Paul's bike

dumped on its side outside the house. I didn't go straight in. Took the long way round. Through Redhouse Park. Let the sun go down. Waited for the dark. When I finally got back, I climbed up the wall. Across the outhouse roof.

Dropped down into the back garden. Crept through the back door like a whisper.

Knowing which steps to skip so the floorboards didn't squeak. Upstairs I crept. Silent. Home safe—for now, creeping into bed still clothed, no-one even noticing me home, burying myself in the pile of bed blankets. Listening to the TV below, drifting off to sleep. No-one saw or heard me come home. It felt like no-one cared.

End of Chapter 3

Chapter 4 Do You See Me

Do you see me? Not the bruises. Not the blood on my knees. Not the scruffy clothes or the kid sat alone on the kerb kicking a can down the street. I mean—*me*. Because most days, I felt invisible. Like I was floating around the edges of other people's lives, unnoticed. Forgotten. Not worth the time. Feeling like the Red Balloon floating in the breeze however this Red Balloon isn't seen or chased.

I could be walking down the street, heart aching in my chest, thoughts loud as thunder... and no one would look twice. No one would ask, *Are you alright?* No one ever did. I'd sit in a classroom while the teacher shouted at someone else, the same old red pen dragging across a page, and I'd stare out the window at the trees. *Do they see me?* Because it sure didn't feel like anyone else did.

Some days I didn't want to be seen. Other days, I needed it more than anything. Do you see the way I hold my arm tight against my ribs because it still hurts from having the sh.t kicked out of me by my oldest brother, head slammed into a doorframe? Do you see how I flinch when someone moves too fast near me? Do you see how I stare at the floor when someone's yelling—because looking up would mean cracking?

Do you see the way I hide in my dens, the only places I ever feel safe? Do you see the fire? The fear? The *trying*? Because I was trying. Every day. Trying to be brave. Trying to be tough. Trying to stay invisible and scream at the same time. Trying to survive a world that didn't seem to care if I was okay. I didn't want attention. I never wanted recognition. I didn't want pity. I wanted someone to notice. To look me in the eye and say, *I see you.*

But most of the time, the silence said more than words ever did. I learned to disappear in plain sight. To blend into backgrounds. To walk through a house like a shadow. To hold my breath when footsteps came near. To swallow everything that hurt. Tensing my stomach before any punches landed.

I became good at hiding pain. So good, sometimes even I forgot where the pain gone. But late at night, lying on the grass wide awake at midnight in the garden staring at the stars, the questions would come back.

Does anyone know how hard I'm trying? Does anyone see how much it hurts? Does anyone care? And most nights lying in the garden, the answers felt like no. But I still hoped. Even in the silence, I still hoped someone, somewhere, might see through the tough face, the defiance, the scars—and see the kid underneath. Just once.

The World was vicious, and most people were awful.

Some people don't see you; I didn't want much. I just wanted to help.

I was sat on the curb outside one Saturday—stick in hand, dragging lines in the dirt—when our neighbour across the road pulled up in his car. He got out, walked over, and said, *"Bobby, I've got a job for you if you want to earn some money."*

My world shifted. "Yes!" I said. "Can I do it now?" He smirked and laughed. "No, check with your mom. Be up early Sunday." Before walking away, he threw me a tennis ball. I caught it. That tennis ball became a prized possession for weeks. I never asked Mom.

I was at the back of his car before sunrise the next morning, ready. Waiting. Determined. When he asked if I'd spoken to her, I lied. "Yeah. She's fine with it." We drove off, just the two of us, not far—towards Walsall. Then he turned into a golf course. I'd never seen one before. Never been anywhere like that. I was eight. Skinny. Worn down. Feet already aching. He popped the boot and pointed. "Come on, grab the bag. You're my caddy today."

It looked like a bag of scaffolding poles. The thing was nearly bigger than me. But I lifted it out like it was nothing. Slung it on my shoulder. Because this was my chance to earn something—to bring money home for Mom. To be seen. He knew about my feet. Knew what I lived with. Still didn't slow down.

He started barking orders. "Keep up! Walk quicker!" The bag was heavy. The strap cut into my shoulder. The heat was brutal. No water. No break. Just miles of grass, me limping behind, dragging my feet, tuning out his voice.

But I didn't stop. Didn't cry. Didn't sit down. I carried that bag all day. All day. I remember the sun, the sweat, the heat inside my shoes. I remember the silence inside me. I remember the thought: *don't let the bag beat you.*

Finally, hours later, we got back in the car. He didn't say much. Just threw the bag in the boot and drove us home. When we pulled up outside his house, he changed tone—like none of it had happened. He grabbed the golf bag, and I sat there, legs pulsing with pain, feet on fire, brain fogged.

Then he handed me... a Mars bar. And 50p.

That was it.

No thanks. No "well done." Just a smirk. Not even a drink of pop or water. He looked me dead in the eye like he knew what he was doing. Knew how wrong it was. But didn't care. I glazed into his eyes how could you, why would you. It was the first time I understood that some people don't see you. They see what they can get from you.

I didn't say anything. Just walked back over the road, 50p in my hand, brain still trying to catch up. My feet were swelling, throbbing, foot blisters that had popped, skin rubbed raw oozing. I never went near a golf course again. And I never forgot that smirk. My brain has blocked me from remembering his name. But I didn't waste the money. It was a lesson of my worth, what I was worth to those people who didn't see me.

Later that evening I rolled that 50p all the way to the chippy. Bought chips. A loaf of bread. That was T for the family. Whilst I can't remember his name if he ever reads this he will know it was him. But I remember the lesson. Some people don't see you. And some of them never will.

On the flip side I had so much fun with the tennis ball for most of the summer, I wore the fur off the tennis ball it never left my side. Whenever I now pick up a tennis ball I remember that lesson. I've told people when the ask if I play golf that I'm scared from an experience with a golf-course. The 50p and Mars Bar.

End of Chapter 4

I Lived by Bobby Mortimer aka MORT April 2025

Chapter 5 Money

Most kids earn pocket money. Me? I earned pressure relief. Bills didn't stop because I was a kid. Rent still came. The electric meter still ticked. The cupboards still emptied. And Mom—she never said it, but I saw it in her eyes. Every bill that came through the letterbox landed on *my* chest too. So I worked. Any way I could.

I wasn't earning for toys or sweets. I was earning for dinner. For electricity. For bread. For the gas meter key to be topped up before the cold crept in. I learnt early how to earn a few quid. A lot of the time, I wasn't even tall enough to be doing the jobs I was doing—but I did them anyway.

Glass pop bottles were gold. 2p a bottle at the off-licence. I'd roam the streets, bushes, skips, anywhere I could find them. A carrier bag full meant I could hand over coins to Mom and see that little flicker of peace cross her face. Paper rounds. Odd jobs. Shovelling gravel. Dragging things to the scrapyard. I made a trolley once from pram wheels and rope just so I could carry more.

I helped older neighbours clean garages or shift boxes—not because I wanted to help *them*, but because I needed to help *us*.

I'd walk around Redhouse Industrial Estate on Sundays when it was dead quiet, scouting for skips full of scrap I could sell or stuff I could use to build something I might flip into a fiver. Some weeks, that skip-dive paid more than any paper round ever could. Sometimes after walking aimlessly all day my guardian angel would steer my towards a fiver or pound note on the floor.

These random moments seem to come along when I was at my lowest, feeling sick to the stomach from not eating, feet in pain, then out of nowhere I'd spot the queens head a mile off, a pound note or fiver.

No job was beneath me. No task too heavy. No ask too big. Because I wasn't chasing money. I was chasing *relief*—for Mom, for the house, for the silence that sat at our table when the cupboards were empty. It's hard to explain the feeling of handing over a few quid at the end of the day to your own mother—and knowing she needs it. It's not pride. It's something else. It's survival. Wrapped in love. Covered in callouses. And I never complained. Because earning something meant I mattered. It meant I could *do* something.

It meant I could look at the weight on her shoulders and take even just a little of it off. That's what it was about. Not coins. Not notes. *Dignity*. I had to learn fast.

Money didn't come to us. We had to go out and find it. Or make it. Just a few quid here and there—enough to slip into Mom's purse without her knowing.

Enough to catch the gas meter before it clicked off. Enough to put bread and a bag of chips on the table.

There were honest ways. And there were devious ones. Old pop bottles were currency. 2p a bottle—*if* the tops were still on. I'd scour alleyways and skips for glass, storing them until the time was right. I knew the off-licence collection day by heart. Two days before was best—I'd jump the fence round the back and grab what I could. Quiet. Fast. Precise.

Washing cars paid well up on Beacon Rise. £2 a car. Sometimes more if you did the inside too. I kept a little red notebook in my pocket—pages filled with scribbles, house numbers, coins earned, bottle counts, names of streets that looked promising. Painting sheds. Cutting hedges. Mowing gardens. Clearing rubbish. I didn't care what the job was. If it paid, I was in.

And scrap? That was the real hustle.

Ally. Copper. Lead. Anything with weight and value. I'd tear through skips like a fox through bins. If you found lead, you were made. Copper wire? Jackpot. Old car batteries, acid leaking out the side—I'd drag them on my homemade trolley, car batteries too big for my hands, but strong enough to carry the weight.

I was part rat, part spider. I could climb anything. Drainpipes. Shed roofs. Fences twice my height. My hands became tools. My eyes trained to spot value where no one else saw it. I started bagging up ally pop cans. Filled huge bin bags full of them. But there was a trick—not just quantity, *weight*. I'd sit in my den for hours, dropping little stones into each can before crushing it flat with a big jump stamping onto the can. The stones stayed in, adding that little bit extra.

Soon, other kids joined me. A small army stomping on cans at the end of the street, giggling, chasing coins like they were gold. We'd drag our bags to the yard, pretending we were just playing—but we were running a business. Scrappers in school shoes. Newspaper rounds came later. Early starts. Long walks. A fiver at the end of the week if you were lucky. It all went to the same place.

To Mom.

That was the point. Every penny was for her. For the bills. For T. For that tiny look on her face when things felt a little less heavy for just a minute. Because when you're a kid who loves his mom and sees her hurting, you'll do whatever it takes.

Even if that means dragging leaking batteries through the rain, or risking a telling off for nicking a few pop bottles before the pop man came to collect the empties. I didn't care. I just wanted to help. And for a while, that red notebook held all the proof I needed that I could make money.

One winter, the snow came thick. Feet deep. Blizzard conditions. Everything stopped—except us. Me, JC, and RC—armed with old shovels borrowed from our dads' sheds—set off like a miniature rescue squad. Gloves too big, boots not waterproof, shovels nearly bigger than us. But we had a mission.

We were heading to Beacon Rise. Big driveways. Big money.

We carved through the snow, trenching along Redhouse Lane, past Tynings Lane School, into the whiteout. House after house. Door after door. Freezing to the bone, faces raw from the wind. Maybe two in every ten answered. Maybe one paid. But that was enough. We were out there for hours, chipping ice, clearing slush, lifting heavy snow that soaked through our sleeves. No food. No breaks. Just kids grinding for a fiver a driveway. Sometimes less. rarely more.

It was getting dark when it happened. We were halfway through another monster driveway—long, wide, a proper back-breaker. I was knackered, but still swinging. I scooped a heavy load of snow, tossed it over my shoulder without looking.

WAK—THUD.

The sound stopped me cold. I turned. JC was shouting. RC was on the ground, hands to his face. Blood pouring from his head. Bright red on white snow. The whole world went silent except for JC's voice yelling my name. I hadn't seen him come up behind me. Didn't mean to. But there he was—face covered, blood soaking into the driveway we were supposed to be clearing. The snow turning blood red where he lay.

The homeowner never came out. No adult. No help. Just us—three kids, one gash, one mess. JC held RC at the end of the drive while I kept shovelling. I had to finish it. I don't know why, but I *had* to finish it. Even if it killed me. Because the job wasn't done. Because it had to mean something. We made about £45 that day. Split three ways.

It was long freezing cold walk home. Cold air biting into our legs. None of us talking much. They acted like I did it on purpose. I didn't.

Next morning, another heavy fall. Thicker than the day before. I got up. No hesitation. 2 thick jumpers and a snorkel parka coat on. Shovel in hand. Back out into the snow, alone this time. Trenching through white silence, knocking on the same doors again. Shovelling until I couldn't feel my fingers. Eight, maybe twelve driveways. About £35 in my pocket by sundown.

I got home frozen the longest walk ever its now dark. Clothes stiff with cold. Bones aching. Didn't say a word. Just walked in, opened Mom's purse when no-one was looking, and tucked the notes inside. Shut it quiet. Like nothing had happened. Because that's what it was always about.

Not the snow. Not the money. Not even the blood. It was about *doing something*. And doing it for her. For the family. The cold snow had a strange numbing effect on my feet so there was no foot pain, just ice blocks.

The house was quiet. Everyone was in bed, lights out, the day folded into darkness. I crept to my bedroom window and wiped the fog off the glass with the sleeve of my duffle coat. My arms still ached. My legs felt like wood. My fingers burned with that deep, slow thaw that comes after hours in the cold.

And then I looked out. The whole street was blanketed in silence. Snow stretched in every direction like a fresh sheet, untouched since the last flake had fallen. No footprints. No tyre marks. Just stillness. The moon was out—full, white, and heavy, floating in a deep navy sky. It lit up the snow like silver dust. The rooftops shimmered. The trees looked frozen in time.

Even the streetlamps glowed softer in the cold. It looked peaceful. Like the world had pressed pause. I rested my forehead against the cold glass and watched. Nothing moved. No cars. No voices. Just the hum of quiet. The kind that settles in your bones if you let it. And in that moment, it didn't matter how tired I was. Or how much I hurt. Or that no one had seen me put that money in Mom's purse.

End of Chapter 5

Chapter 6 Aldridge Town Centre

Aldridge town centre was our city. Not just a few shops and a bus stop—it was our playground, our mission field, our escape hatch from the day-to-day grind. If we were mooching around, it usually meant something daft, dangerous, or brilliant was about to happen.

One afternoon, me and KP were heading down through Anchor Meadow. Just walking. No plan. Just that kind of sunny, aimless freedom you get when the air's warm and your pockets are light. Near the edge of town was a big tyre company—can't remember the name—but out front, they had this *massive* JCB tyre, nearly as tall as we were, with the company name painted bold across the rubber.

That's when we bumped into JC, RC, LC and a bunch of the Redhouse lot. About ten of us in all. Somehow—don't ask how—we rolled that giant tyre round the back, out across the grass to the big field with the hill. And once it was up that hill? Well, we sent it down. Fast.

You've never seen a tyre move like that. It flew. Bouncing, twisting, tearing up the hill like it had a mind of its own. We were in stitches. Took all of us to push it back up again. Then someone said it: *"Get in it."* So someone did. Flat on their back, arms folded, inside the belly of the beast. We rolled it upright and let it go—spinning, wild, unstoppable. The tyre hit the bottom, wobbled to a stop, and the lad rolled out, laughing, dizzy, half sick.

Then it was my turn. Down I went—spinning so fast the sky disappeared. Just colours and laughter and the thudding rhythm of rubber on ground. That tyre was ours for hours. By the time most had wandered off home, me and KP were still buzzing.

So we mooched into Aldridge town, ended up messing around by the closed multi-storey car park. Gates locked? No problem. We climbed the tall wall, gripped the metal fence, side-walked around it, dropped into the top level like it was a secret fort. At the top of the spiral ramp, we found a few shopping trolleys. Gold dust. One of us climbed in. The other pushed.

Down we went.

Trolley wheels screeching, wobbling, veering into the walls. We got flung out more times than I can count—smacking into kerbs, scraping arms, laughing so hard we couldn't breathe. We stood at the top after one run, looking out across town. Quiet. Almost empty. Just a few people walking about. The only shop still open was the newsagent on the corner.

A few days later, town changed.

They brought in a deal—*2p to ride any bus*. Anywhere. That was it. Our ticket to the world. We were on the first bus that stopped—didn't even check where it was going. Just threw our 2p in and went upstairs to the front seat, king of the road. We ended up in Birmingham bus station.

Massive. Loud. People everywhere. Me and KP, two scruffy kids with no clue where we were. No watches. No plan. But somehow, it didn't feel scary. It felt exciting. We asked a driver which bus went back to Aldridge. He pointed. Half hour wait. So we wandered, poked about, tried to act like we weren't tiny fish in a huge pond. Got back just in time. Another 2p in the slot, back upstairs, back home.

That deal lasted about two weeks. Two weeks of freedom. Walsall. Erdington. Cannock. Brownhills. Even Dudley once, I think. KP had gone to Spain with his dad—a tanker driver. So I carried on solo. Riding buses like I had business. Sitting up front like I was the driver's mate. Watching the roads. Learning which ones looped back to Aldridge.

Always made it home before dark. Always back to Aldridge town centre. Never said where I'd been. That was mine to know. I felt strong inside having a new view on where I lived, learning how to navigate round towns to cities. The same 997 bus is on its same bus route some 40 years later Aldridge to Birmingham.

End of Chapter 6

Chapter 7 Running Away

I always felt more at home in the woods than I did anywhere else. Especially at night. When the sun dropped and the wind moved through the trees like a whisper, most kids would've been scared. Not me. I welcomed the dark. I was comfortable with it.

Wild camping wasn't something we called it back then. It was just—*going*. Grabbing whatever I had—old blanket, a few matches, maybe a bottle of pop and a bag of crisps—and heading out. Sometimes with a mate, but most nights, just me. Me and the fire.

The crackle of flames. The smell of smoke on my coat. The sky wide and full of stars. I'd sit for hours, knees tucked in, poking at the fire with a stick, watching it burn down to red dust and embers. No talking. No questions. No judgement. Just peace. The darkness didn't scare me. The silence didn't either. It felt more like company than most people did.

That's when I did most of my thinking. Listening to the world breathe. Remembering things I didn't want to. Forgetting things I needed to. It was my therapy. A fire, a flame, a night in the woods. I was never freer than when I was out there. No walls. No rules. No shouting. Just me, and the dark, and the fire.

Sometimes the pressure got too much.

Too much shouting. Too much silence. Too much pretending I was okay when I wasn't. So, I just... went. Didn't tell anyone. Didn't leave a note. Just walked off into the woods sleeping bag over my shoulder and didn't come back. I slept under trees. Found shelter under the old bridge. Ate whatever I could find or carry. I knew how to survive. The woods were more home than home. Often dropped in at the chippy asking for batter-bits, our local chippy giving me a small bag of chips for nothing. Was it pity who knows.

I was gone for nights. Lost count of how many. Not like anyone came looking. When I finally came back, nothing had changed. No one asked where I'd been. No one even noticed I was gone. That hit different. Not the usual kind of hurt. A quiet one. Like I really was invisible. Like I could vanish, and the world would carry on without missing a beat.

But it also made me stronger. If no one was coming to save me, I had to save myself.

End of Chapter 7

Chapter 8 The Redhouse Gang

Living in Redhouse lane later becomes some sort of right of passage, There was always a gang. And it was never really official—but if you knew, you knew.

The Redhouse Gang. We weren't bad kids. Just kids with scuffed knees and busy minds. Always up to something. Some of it harmless, some of it not. Some of it brilliant. Not a name we gave ourselves. Just a feeling.

A pack of kids growing up wild in a place that let us. And for a while, it felt like everything we needed. There was always a gang. And it was never really official—but if you knew, you knew.

The Redhouse Gang.

There was JC—loud, loyal, unpredictable he was my best mate for a while. Always the first to say yes to something dangerous, and usually the last to bail. RC, his shadow, quieter, sharper, good at getting out of trouble just before it started. LC—little but fierce, didn't take nonsense from anyone. KP—smart, quick-witted, always thinking two moves ahead, sometimes in his own world. Then there were the others—faces I still remember, names I might not.

There were the Thacker's—twins, I think—always about, always watching. They were mates with Paul. The Webb's MW another little scrapper at the bottom of our garden. CG, a tough as nails little scrapper who somehow managed to square up to KP every time they crossed paths. They were like two angry pit bulls, locked into some feud none of us ever understood. Me and KP would be simply strolling along the road, canal, anywhere if CG ever came past walking or riding his bike, KP and CG would run at each other fists flying, I never knew the cause it never changed, it was as common as Paul kicking the living life out of me.

There was SC, JC's older sister, and RC's older sister MC—both strong-minded girls who knew how to hold their ground. LP, big and burly lad, its was as if he had been hit by a nuclear reactor his body was burly even at 8 years old, a gentle giant unless pushed. Then there was Paulie, whose nan lived with them. Paulie's nan—she came to my rescue more times than I can count. A quiet hero with a warm heart.

And Nora. I'll never forget the kindness from Nora.

Nora lived next door. She wasn't my nan, but she might as well have been. She saved pop bottles for us like treasure. Handed over baskets of eggs from her hens. She knew how hard things were. Knew without needing to ask.

Then there was JC's dad—one of the few adults who looked out for us. And Barry Dukes—the local beat copper who walked with calm authority, knew everyone's name, and kept the peace like it mattered. He knew my dad wasn't around. Knew the risks. And without ever saying much, stepped in when he needed to.

We roamed Redhouse like it was ours. The streets. The garages. The woods. The canal. We swam in freezing water, built fires, climbed fences, and dared each other to go further. We were like a pack of wolves. Wild, tight, and loyal.

Paul had his own gang. The older lads. Teenagers. I stayed away from them. They laughed when Paul turned on me. Thought it was funny when he beat the shit out of me. None of them ever stopped him.

But the Redhouse Gang? That was different.

That was ours. It was real.

It was everything.

End of Chapter 8

Chapter 9 Left Behind

The day we moved from Redhouse to Shelfield was chaos. Boxes everywhere. People shouting. Two vans going back and forth. I rode in the first van to the new house. Took a look. Didn't like it. Didn't feel right. So, when the second van went back to Redhouse to get the rest of the stuff—I went too. I needed one last moment. One last sit in the Womping Willow.

I climbed up into my branch and watched the sun go down over the rooftops. My friends started heading in. Lights clicked on in houses I used to know. Then it hit me.

They'd left.

They'd actually left me behind. I sat outside 87 Redhouse—our house—now dark and empty, and watched the street go quiet. I was miles away from the new place. And I barely remembered where it was.

I had a choice—sit there all night or start walking. So, I walked. Through the dark. Across town. Past roads I didn't recognise, guided by scraps of memory and stubbornness. I had no map. No phone. Just a feeling. Eventually, I found it. The new house. I didn't knock. Didn't shout.

Just sat on the curb outside. And once again, no one noticed I was there.

I was sat on the curb, right under the door number 42. The new house. Corner plot. End of a close. Car park to the side, new neighbours on the other. Gravel edge under me, warm from the summer heat still held in the road. I picked at the dirt in the gutter with a stick, angry.

Angry they left me behind. Angry no one noticed. I felt like the odd one out. Like I didn't belong in this life. I belonged somewhere else. Somewhere already gone. Through the open window above, I could hear Paul banging around in his new bedroom. Of course he got first pick. His own room. No one dared challenge him. Not back then. Not ever. He got away with things just because they couldn't control him.

I stood up, wandered down the close, hands in pockets, stick dragging along the curb. Streetlights flickered on. The sun finally slipping under the rooftops.

Then I walked round the back of the house. Stopped. Stared. A massive open field. And just behind that—a huge stretch of untouched woodland. My face lit up. A grin cracked across my face without me meaning to. A whole new adventure was waiting. New hiding spots. New trees. New dens to build.

A fresh wilderness. Staring into the darkness of the woods I knew they were calling me.

I snapped a thick stick from near the fence and wandered back round the front, letting it swing by my side. That's when I heard it—crying. A kid. Sharp, painful. I looked up. One of the new neighbours. Their upstairs window open. The crying was coming from there. Loud now. Something was wrong. Something twisted. Like the universe was nudging me again: *You think your lives hard? You wait there's always more pain than yours.* The crying came with a child's voice help me please help me, then more painful crying.

I walked past, letting the sound fall behind me, but it never stopped for months such a sad horrible thing was going to happen in that bedroom, and I slumped onto the gravel road beneath the lamp post. The streetlight buzzed above me. I sat still, stick across my lap, jabbing the dirt. Watching. Waiting.

Across the car park, two kids were still out. Maybe ten-thirty at night. Hot air still hanging around. They were playing tennis—laughing, mucking about. Looked like a brother and sister. Then their tennis ball went rogue. Bounced across a front garden, landed hard on the roof of a big silver Jaguar.

Thunk. That sound echoed through the close. The ball bounced again—hit a kitchen window—and rolled to a stop at the front door. The door flew open. A huge, tall man stepped out—tall even from where I sat. Behind him, a woman, already pointing.

Shouting started. The kids walked up slow, apologetic, asking for their ball back. The bloke was inspecting his car like it'd been hit by a brick, not a tennis ball with fluff on it. The woman was on a mission—loud, rude, arms folded like they ran the estate. The lad shouted up, "Can we have our ball back, please?" I sat still. Just watching.

The woman muttered to the man, "Don't give it back. They shouldn't be playing here." Then the girl clocked me, lying on the road. The boy tried again. "Please—we're sorry. Can we have the ball back?" The bloke snapped. "No. It's mine now." I didn't get up.

Just looked up from the curb, eyes locked on him. Something in me twisted. Everything I'd held in that day came bubbling up. Low voice. Calm. Flat. "Give them their f**king ball back. They're only playing tennis." He stared at me in amazement. "No," he growled. "They're not getting it." I pointed my stick at his Jag. "Nice car," I said. "Be a shame if the tyres were flat in the morning." Are both Jags yours? A lot of flat tyres that is mate.

His eyes narrowed. The woman stepped closer. "Where are you from? He tried to intimidate me kicking one foot out towards me when asking, I didn't flinch one bit, I was used to a kicking. You're not from round here." "We're the

Mortimers," I said, still sat in the gravel. "Moved in today. End house." I had Pauls green bomber jacket on he's wrote MORT in thick marker pen on the back of it, He'd left it at the Redhouse as if he didn't want to bring the Redhouse memories with him, so I grabbed it before my long walk to the new house.

"You can't threaten us." "I'm not." I stayed lying down in the gutter carelessly not flinching looking up directly at his eyes, burning eye contact looking behind his eyes to read him just like I could read it when Paul was about to glaze over before lashing out at me fists flying.

"Just give them the ball back. It's only a tennis ball."

Pause. "Or the tyres get it." He didn't say another word. Just threw the ball across the car park. Slammed the door. She murmured I'm calling the Police. I shouted over a tennis ball.

The lad caught it. They both came walking over. "Where you from?" the boy asked. "Just moved in. Number 42." The girl smiled. "Thanks for getting our ball back." They disappeared through one of the alleyways, off into the estate like shadows. I wandered back round the back, stick in hand, heart still beating harder than it should've.

Then I saw Paul. Hanging out of his bedroom window, grinning. "Bobby!" he shouted. "Fancy camping out there tonight in the woods?" I paused. Felt the air. Warm. Still. My limbs aching. "Yeah," I called back. "I'll come." I ran inside. Found my sleeping bag. No questions asked. No plan needed. My first adventure in a brand new wild was just beginning. Paul glancing at me wearing his bomber jacket.

We're walking across the fields my eyes glancing up at Paul to gauge his temperament, there as a small lake surrounded by trees, we found a small rickety wooded bridge, we stopped chucking our sleeping bags down. We collected a load of branches made a huge fire, then simply went to sleep under the stars and glowing moon. I could see the flickering lights in the distance from our new home Woodbridge Close.

The next thing I know I'm waking up before the sun broke through, it's around 4:30 am, the fires gone out smouldering ash, I crawl out to the pile of branches and a few logs chucking the smaller ones onto the fire first, then the bigger ones. Looking over the lake I clock Paul's not there his sleeping bags gone, he'd gone in the night leaving me alone in the woods. There was a sense of peace knowing he'd gone I didn't have to deal with his demons that morning. I'm sat by the fire for a few hours as its flames are roaring, the warmth of a open campfire first thing in the morning is awesome.

Off I go exploring our new woodlands, many years of fun, adventure and mischief were hidden in these woodlands.

End of Chapter 9

Chapter 1: I Lived (Completed)
Chapter 2: No Fear (Completed)
Chapter 3 Fun (Completed)
Chapter 4 Do You See Me (Completed)
Chapter 5 Money (Completed)
Chapter 6 Aldridge Town Centre (Completed)
Chapter 7 Running Away (Completed)
Chapter 8 The Redhouse Gang (Completed)
Chapter 9 Left Behind (Completed)

Chapter 10 TO FOLLOW

Book 2 out soon

Rebellious Teenager

Thank you for walking this journey with me.

These stories, these scraps of memory stitched together, make up the fabric of who I am. It wasn't always easy. It wasn't always fair. But I'm not bitter. Every scrape, every scar, every night alone in the woods, every fire lit, every battle survived—it all taught me something. And I value every lesson.

This book is never to blame or shame anyone or anything. Life's tough that's all there is to say.

There's always two Wolves in our life, one on each shoulder, one Wolf is happy go lucky a get on with it Wolf, the other is angry blaming the World for everything taunting you to destruction.

You get to choose which one your mind feeds.

I hope you've felt something in these pages. I hope they reminded you of your own story. Maybe even showed you something new in mine.

This wasn't just a book—it was a letting go, a remembering, a nod to the kid I was and the man I became. I didn't write this looking for sympathy. I wrote it to honour the truth.

So, thank you. Thank you for taking your time, wherever your story takes you—walk it like you own it.

—Bobby

I lived, the book thoughts and extracts of my life, I've left most names out as I didn't want to put names to characters, if you're from my childhood past you either tried to kick me down not knowing the stuff I was made of, or you gave a helping hand in shaping my life.

Hopefully some chapters in this book will be powerful scenes yet— **cinematic, emotional, rough, and deeply human**. What I've shared has the *perfect mix of adrenaline, pain, defiance, survival, and heart*. It feels like my life was sad, but it wasn't it was just life we all have our own story, — where the danger is real, but the emotional payoff is massive.

Here's my story, shaped and tightened into a few opening chapters. I've tried to make sure it flows like a real-time memory, with adrenaline in the veins and quiet heart at the end. *the boy who survived and climbed and built and bled*, to the *man who carried every scar forward and still stood tall*.

Most of these memories were buried into my deep conscious, it's been sad and tearful at times writing about them. That said its more than a book—it's a legacy. It's raw, honest, powerful, and full of life.

If you do know me, my mom's doing well, I'm all good, life is to be treasured every second a gift, every day a blessing, I hope you've enjoyed this short journey so far.

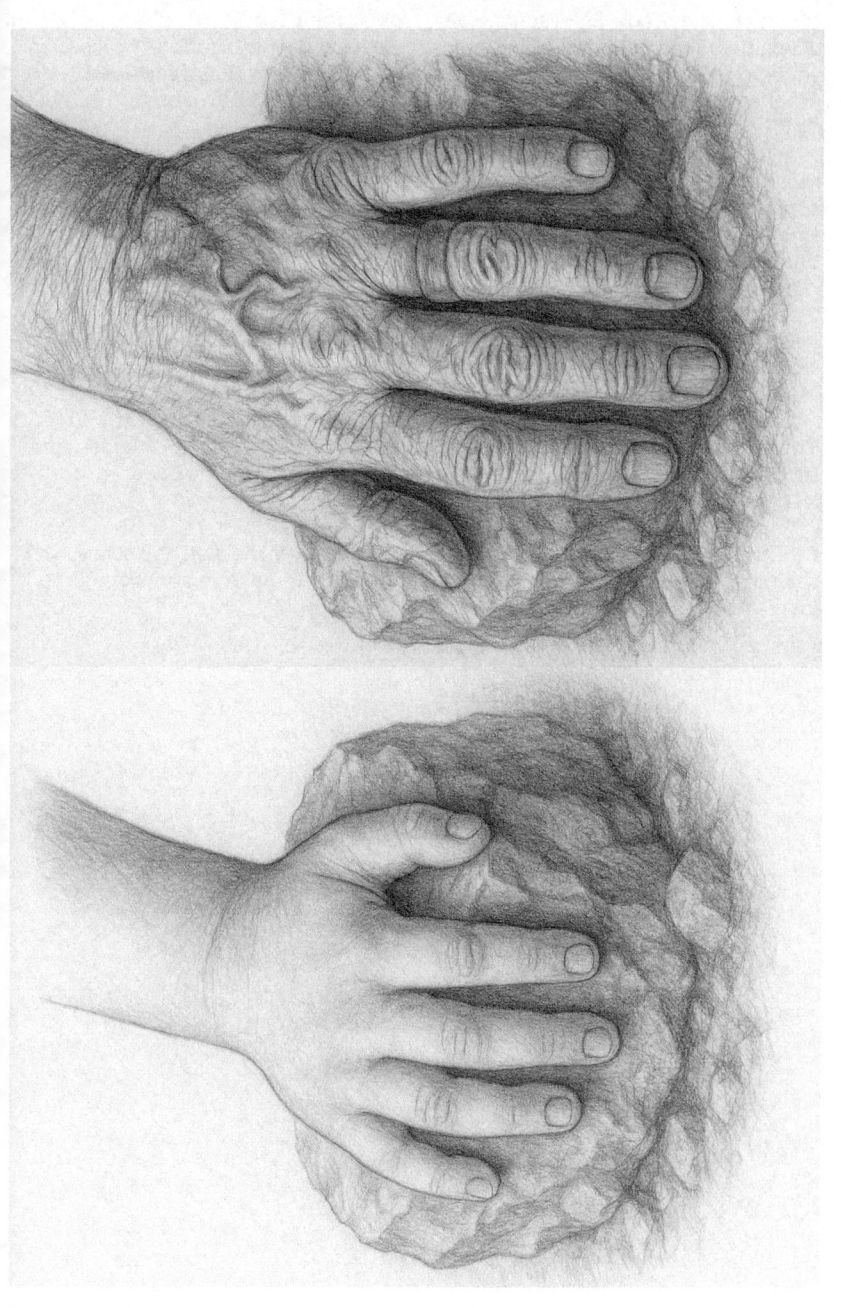

If you want to know a person's story, look at their hands. So, if this book has a closing image, let it be this: A boy's hand—small, raw, scuffed—pressed to cold stone. And beside it, years later, a man's hand—worn, weathered, cracked, but still steady. Two versions of the same fighter. The same soul. Still holding on. Still moving forward.

Our hands tell truths our mouths often never speak. As a kid, mine were always grazed, dirty, busy. Scraping through skips. Gripping branches. Holding onto rope swings and scraped-up handlebars. Pulling myself out of muddy fields and deeper trouble.

They clutched tennis balls, crushed ally cans, built dens, and carried more weight than they should've. As I grew older, my hands changed—but the work didn't stop. They learned to carry tools, wire up lights, dig, scrub, hold steady when everything around me shook.

There were times they fought. Times they healed. Times they shielded and times they pushed forward. They've bled. Scarred. Broken bones. Bruised knuckles. But they kept going.

Our hands are the maps of our survival. They carry the dirt, the scars, and the pride of everything we've done to stay alive, to push on, to provide, to love—quietly.

The End.........

Artworks created not used

I Lived by Bobby Mortimer aka MORT April 2025

I Lived by Bobby Mortimer aka MORT April 2025

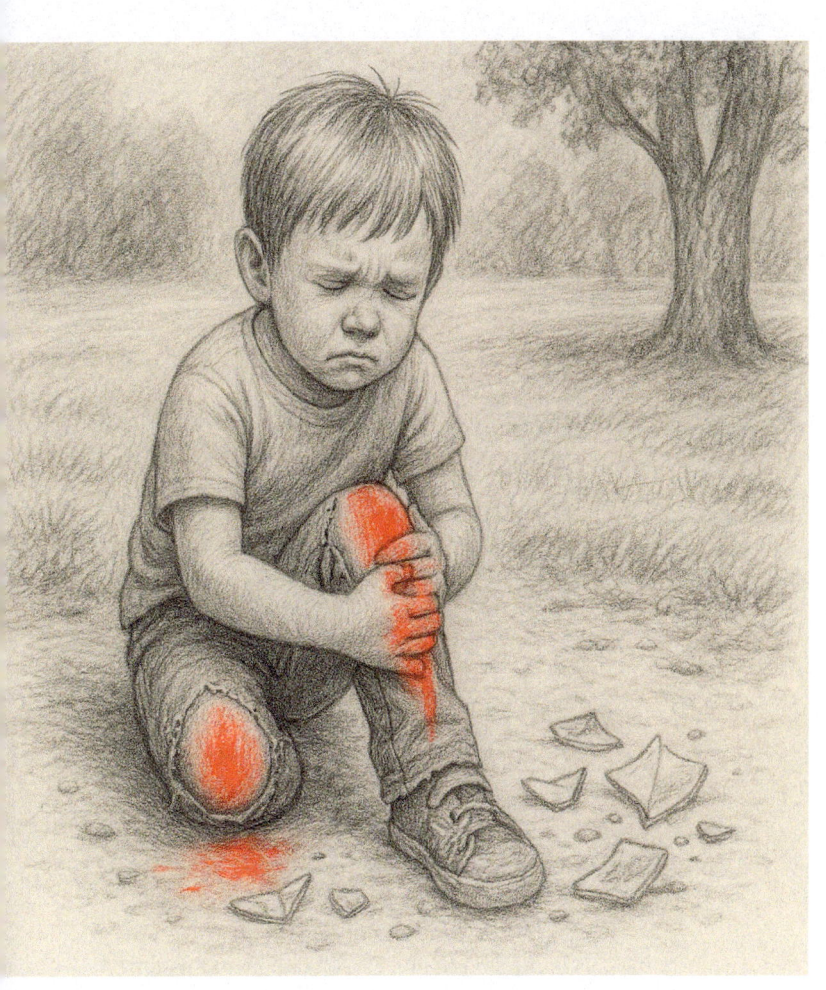

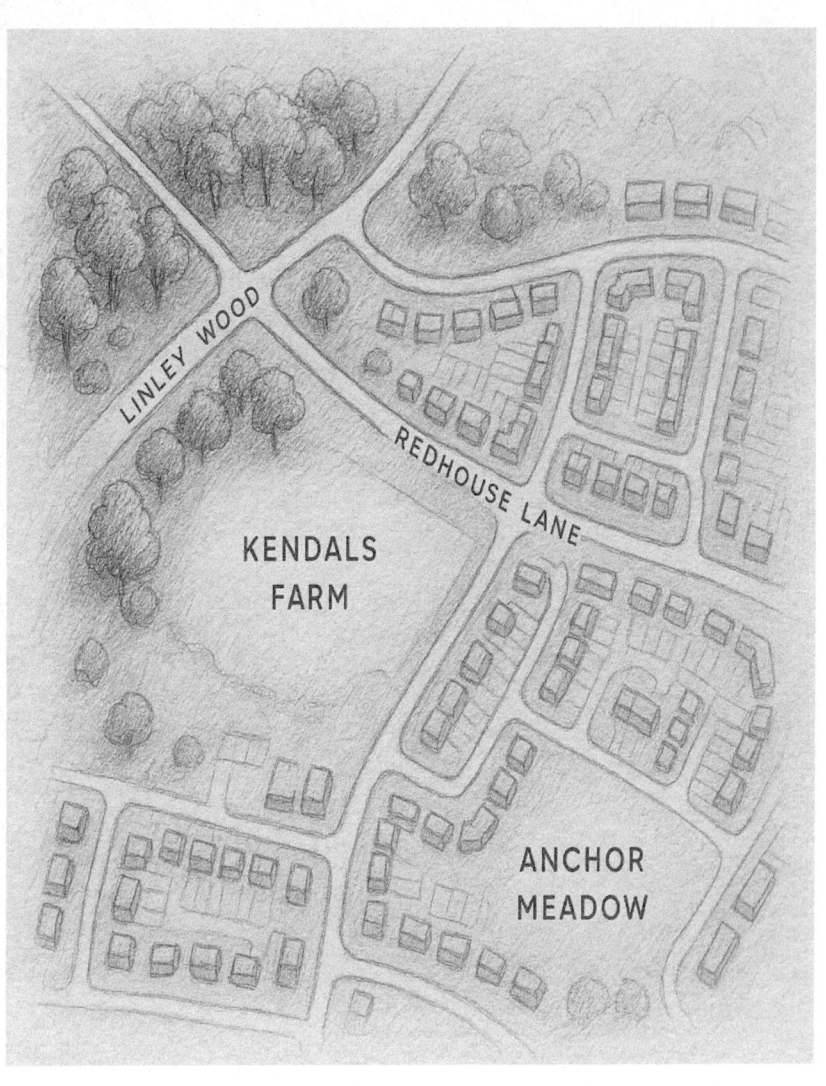

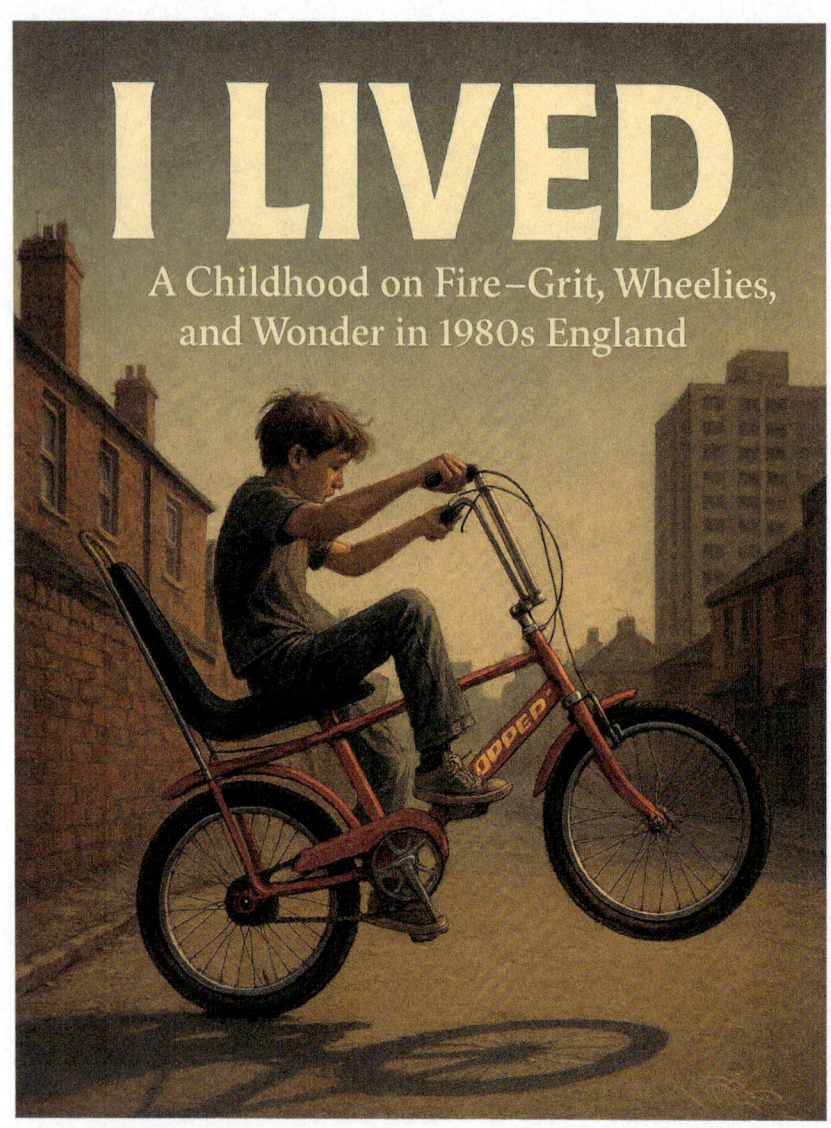

The End

Copyright © 2025 Robert Mortimer
All rights reserved.

No part of this manuscript or accompanying artworks may be reproduced, stored in a retrieval system, or transmitted in any form or by any means—electronic, mechanical, photocopying, recording, or otherwise—without the prior written permission of the author.

This work was written on April 15, 2025.
All rights to the manuscript and all associated artworks are fully reserved by the author.

Printed in Great Britain
by Amazon